# FULL MOON AND STAR

By LEE BENNETT HOPKINS

Illustrated by MARCELLUS HALL

ABRAMS BOOKS FOR YOUNG READERS
NEW YORK

The illustrations in this book were made with
pen and ink and watercolor on paper.

Cataloging-in-Publication Data has been applied
for and may be obtained from the Library of Congress.
ISBN: 978-1-4197-0013-2

Text copyright © 2011 Lee Bennett Hopkins
Illustrations copyright © 2011 Marcellus Hall

Book design by Chad W. Beckerman

Published in 2011 by Abrams Books for Young Readers, an imprint of ABRAMS.
All rights reserved. No portion of this book may be reproduced, stored in a retrieval
system, or transmitted in any form or by any means, mechanical, electronic,
photocopying, recording, or otherwise, without written permission from the publisher.

Printed and bound in China

10 9 8 7 6 5 4 3 2 1

Abrams Books for Young Readers are available at special discounts when purchased in
quantity for premiums and promotions as well as fundraising or educational use. Special editions
can also be created to specification. For details, contact specialmarkets@abramsbooks.com or the address below.

ABRAMS
THE ART OF BOOKS SINCE 1949
115 West 18th Street
New York, NY 10011
www.abramsbooks.com

To my sister, Donna Lea Venturi,
my favorite leading lady.
—L.B.H.

To Tamar and Chad.
—M.H.

# Act One

Kyle and Katie are best friends.
They do everything together.

One day Kyle told Katie, "I wrote a play."

"But we always do things together," said Katie.

"I just wrote it last night," Kyle said. "Would you like to read it?"

"Sure would," Katie answered.

# ON

## A PLAY BY KYLE

### CAST OF CHARACTERS
- HALF-MOON ONE
- HALF-MOON TWO

(HALF-MOON ONE enters stage right and moves slowly to the middle of the stage.)

HALF-MOON ONE: I am a half-moon.

(HALF-MOON TWO enters stage left.)

HALF-MOON TWO: I am a half-moon, too!

HALF-MOON ONE: If we meet together we will become a full moon.

HALF-MOON TWO: Good idea. Everyone loves a full moon.

(They move together to become a full moon.)

HALF-MOON ONE and HALF-MOON TWO:
  We are now a full, full moon.

HALF-MOON ONE: We look good together.

HALF-MOON TWO: We do. But a full moon
  cannot last forever.

*(HALF-MOON ONE leaves stage right.)*

*(HALF-MOON TWO leaves stage left.)*

# CURTAIN

"Do you like it?" Kyle asked.

"Yes. Yes I do," Katie said. "You wrote a very good play."

# ACT TWO

The next day Kyle and Katie were doing homework together after school at Katie's house.

"I liked your play so much," said Katie, "that I wrote one, too. Would you like to read it?"

"Sure would," Kyle answered.

# STA

## A PLAY BY KATIE

### CAST OF CHARACTERS
- STAR ONE
- STAR TWO

*(STAR ONE and STAR TWO walk onstage. They dance around.)*
STAR ONE and STAR TWO:

Twinkle,                    twinkle,                    twinkle.

Twinkle,                                    twinkle,

twinkle.

Twinkle,                              twinkle,

twinkle.

Twinkle, twinkle. Look at us twinkle. Twinkle, twinkle, twinkle.

*(STAR TWO leaves the stage. STAR ONE remains.)*

STAR ONE: I don't want to twinkle all alone. Will you
come back to light up the night sky with me?

*(STAR TWO comes back. They dance round and round. They take a bow.)*

# CURTAIN

"Do you like it?" Katie asked.

"Yes. Yes I do," Kyle said. "You wrote a very good play."

# ACT THREE

"I have an idea," Katie said.
"You wrote a play about moons.
I wrote a play about stars.
Since we always do things together,
why don't we write a play together, too?"

"What a good idea," Kyle said.
"Let's do it."

Together, Kyle and Katie wrote their play.

(FULL MOON *sits alone onstage on a high stool.*
*STAR enters from stage left.*)

STAR: Good evening, Full Moon. You are so bright tonight.

FULL MOON: You are bright tonight, too, Star.

STAR: I am so lucky to have you hanging around me.

FULL MOON: I am lucky, too. Your twinkle makes me glow with happiness.

STAR: Do you know there have been stories, poems, and songs written about how beautiful you are?

FULL MOON: Did you know there have been stories, poems, and songs written about how beautiful you are, too?

STAR: The thing I like most is that you and I are together every night. I'm never lonely when you're around. I love your graceful glow, Full Moon.

FULL MOON: I love your sparkling twinkle. It reminds me that I always have a friend.

STAR: Glowing is so nice.

FULL MOON: So is twinkling.

FULL MOON and STAR: We will be friends forever.

*(FULL MOON and STAR take each other's hand. They move to center stage and take a bow.)*

CURTAIN

Kyle and Katie read their play over
and over.

"You know what?" Katie asked.

"What?" Kyle said.

"I loved your play about moons. And I
am glad you loved my play about stars.
But best of all I love our play—
*Full Moon and Star*.
Do you know why I love it best?"

"Why?" asked Kyle.

"Because we did it together.
We should always do things together."

"I agree," said Kyle.

"Me, too," said Katie. "Forever."